Parts

For Mike, John, Fred,
Matt, Phil, and Ryan

Keep it together, guys!

Published by Dial Books for Young Readers
A division of Penguin Young Readers Group
345 Hudson Street
New York, New York 10014

Copyright © 1997 by Tedd Arnold
Typography by Nancy R. Leo
Manufactured in China on acid-free paper
First Edition
24 26 28 30 29 27 25

Library of Congress Cataloging in Publication Data
Arnold, Tedd.
Parts / Tedd Arnold.—1st ed.
p.   cm.
Summary: A five-year-old boy thinks his
body is falling apart until he learns new teeth grow, and
hair and skin replace themselves.
ISBN 0-8037-2040-8 (trade).—ISBN 0-8037-2041-6 (lib. bdg.)
[1. Body, Human—Fiction. 2. Stories in rhyme.] I. Title.
PZ8.3.A647Par 1997   [E]—dc20   96-28552   CIP   AC

The art was prepared using color pencils and watercolor washes,
and the text was hand-lettered by Mr. Arnold.

Parts

Tedd Arnold

Dial Books for Young Readers New York

I just don't know what's going on
Or why it has to be.
But every day it's something worse.
What's happening to me?

I think it was three days ago
I first became aware~
That in my comb were caught a couple
Pieces of my hair.

I stared at them, amazed, and more
Than just a bit appalled
To think that I was only five
And starting to go bald!

Then later on (I don't recall
Exactly when it was)
I lifted up my shirt and found
This little piece of fuzz.

I stared at it, amazed, and wondered,
What's this all about?
But then I understood. It was
My stuffing coming out!

Next day when I was outside playing
With the water hose,
I saw that little bits of skin
Were peeling from my toes.

I stared at them, amazed, and then
I gave a little groan,
To think that pretty soon I might
Be peeled down to the bone.

Then yesterday, before my bath,
As I took off my clothes,
A chunk of something gray and wet
Fell right out of my nose.

I stared at it, amazed, and thought,
I should be feeling pain.
Well, wouldn't *you* if you just lost
A little piece of brain?

So now, today, I'm sitting here
Enjoying Dr. Seuss,
And suddenly I realize
A tooth is coming loose!

I wiggle it, amazed, dismayed,
Too horrified to speak.
Without my teeth, how can I eat?
Already I feel weak!

Now I'm really worried. I'm
As scared as I can be,
'Cause finally what's happening
Is very clear to see—

The glue that holds
our parts together
isn't holding me!!!

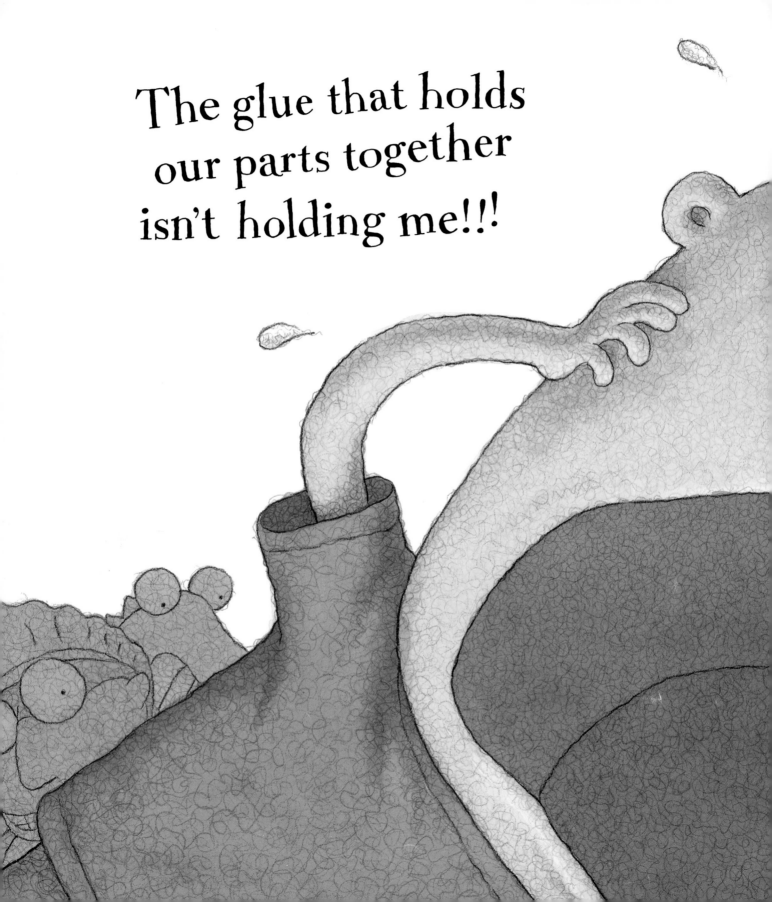

And now I'm thinking to myself,
What's next in line to go?
Might be my ears; might be my eyeballs.
How's a kid to know?

One day I might be playing ball...
And have my arm fall off.

Or maybe I could lose my head
If suddenly I cough.

Quite soon I'll be in pieces in
A pile without a shape.

Thank goodness Dad keeps lots and lots
And lots of masking tape.

What?

You forgot?
   To tell me teeth fall out?
And when they do, some brand-new teeth
   Will soon begin to sprout?

My hair, my skin, and everything—
There's nothing I should fear?

So all of me is normal. Whew!
That's really good to hear!

Then tell me, what's this yellow stuff
I got out of my ear?